What Can I See in the Fall?

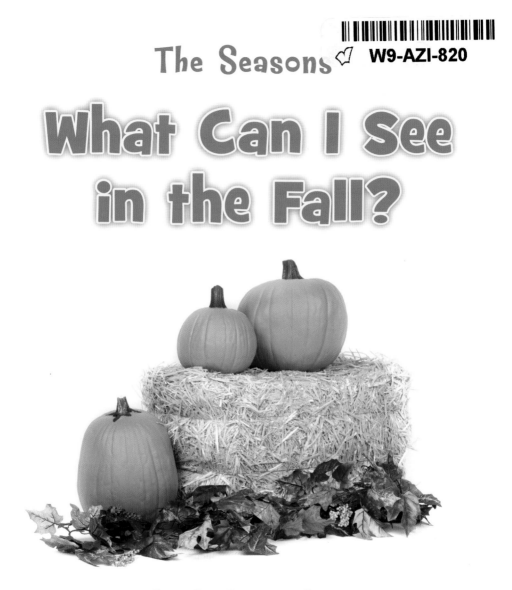

By Cecilia Minden

 It must be fall.

What can I see in the fall?

4   I can see leaves in the fall.

I like to jump in leaves.

I can see apples in the fall.

I like to pick apples.

I can see pumpkins in the fall.

I like to cut up pumpkins.

I can see nuts in the fall.

I like to crack nuts.

 It must be fall.

What can you see in the fall?

Word List

sight words

apples	like	to
be	pumpkins	What
I	see	you
leaves	the	

short a words	short i words	short u words
can	in	cut
crack	pick	jump
fall		must
		nuts
		up

It must be fall.
What can I see in the fall?
I can see leaves in the fall.
I like to jump in leaves.
I can see apples in the fall.
I like to pick apples.
I can see pumpkins in the fall.
I like to cut up pumpkins.
I can see nuts in the fall.
I like to crack nuts.
It must be fall.
What can you see in the fall?

Published in the United States of America by Cherry Lake Publishing
Ann Arbor, Michigan
www.cherrylakepublishing.com

Cherry Blossom Press is an imprint of Cherry Lake Publishing.

Library of Congress Cataloging-in-Publication Data has been filed and is available at catalog.loc.gov

Printed in the United States of America
Corporate Graphics

Cecilia Minden is the former director of the Language and Literacy Program at Harvard Graduate School of Education. She earned her PhD in Reading Education at the University of Virginia. Dr. Minden has written extensively for early readers. She is passionate about matching children to the very book they need to improve their skills and progress to a deeper understanding of all the wonder books can hold. Dr. Minden and her family live in McKinney, Texas.